KU-072-870

FREDDY TANGLES

Champ or Chicken

written by
JACK BRAND
drawings by Tom Jellett

BOLTON LIBRARIES

BT 2091385 0

Thanks for everything, Bearsy.

First published in 2015

Copyright © Text, Jack Brand 2015
Copyright © Illustrations, Tom Jellett 2015

All rights reserved. No part of this book may be reproduced or transmitted
in any form or by any means, electronic or mechanical, including photocopying,
recording or by any information storage and retrieval system, without prior
permission in writing from the publisher. The Australian *Copyright Act* 1968
(the Act) allows a maximum of one chapter or ten per cent of this book, whichever
is the greater, to be photocopied by any educational institution for its educational
purposes provided that the educational institution (or body that administers it) has
given a remuneration notice to the Copyright Agency (Australia) under the Act.

Allen & Unwin
83 Alexander Street
Crows Nest NSW 2065
Phone: (61 2) 8425 0100
Email: info@allenandunwin.com
Web: www.allenandunwin.com

A Cataloguing-in-Publication entry is available from the
National Library of Australia
www.trove.nla.gov.au

ISBN 978 1 76011 035 2

Cover and text design by Liz Seymour
Cover and internal illustrations by Tom Jellett
Set in Dyslexie 9/15 pt by Liz Seymour
This book was printed in Australia in August 2015 at McPherson's Printing Group,
76 Nelson St, Maryborough, Victoria 3465, Australia.

This title has been specifically styled in Dyslexie – a revolutionary font in which each
character has a unique form designed to simplify life for those who have dyslexia.
For more information about Dyslexie, go to dyslexiefont.com.

10 9 8 7 6 5 4 3 2 1

MIX
Paper from
responsible sources
FSC   FSC® C001695

The paper in this book is FSC® certified.
FSC® promotes environmentally responsible,
socially beneficial and economically viable
management of the world's forests.

Tabby was mad, really mad.

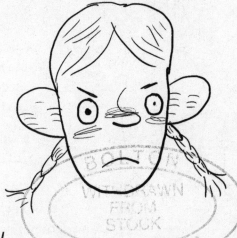

BOLTON WITHDRAWN FROM STOCK LIBRARIES

At me!

'What would you rather be?'
she asked, not very nicely.

I usually liked Tabby's 'what would you rather'
questions. Normally we would all have a say and
a laugh, but not this time. No-one was laughing
or saying anything.

She looks really angry

Yeah ... let's stay away from her feet!

1

Every girl in the playground stood behind her.

It was kind of intense.

My friends Blocker, Scabs and Cooper weren't helping me either. They were absolutely still, like statues, and I knew why too: no-one messed with Tabby when she was this angry.

As you can see from the Tabby Angryometer ...

This tool measures the angriness of Tabby and then supplies useful advice. Right now, the pointer was on Don't even move!

TODAY'S TABBY DANGER

TRY TO · RUN! · DON'T EVEN MOVE

2

Then she asked the question,

'What would you rather be?

'A girl who a stupid boy thinks is a boy even though she is actually a girl?

or

'A girl who a stupid boy thinks is a girl, and actually is a girl?'

Words started falling out of my mouth.

I knew because of the Tabby Angryometer that I shouldn't move and should definitely not say anything, but I couldn't help it. The words just fell out. I didn't know what they were going to be. I was just hoping that when all the words were out and they were stuck together, they would somehow make Tabby less angry at me.

Unfortunately, the words came out in this order.

SORRY Really you Not giRL Umm I said like boy.

It was definitely not the way I was hoping the words would come out and I confirmed that by checking Tabby's face, which was now even angrier.

like Really SORRY
I Umm Said you boy

I quickly shuffled the words around and said it again.

That was better.

Not giRL

Only Tabby didn't care because, as the Tabby Angryometer said, no words could help me when she was this angry.

She shoved the words back into my mouth.

She said,

'No, this is a question for girls to answer, not stupid boys!'

All the girls immediately agreed that a stupid boy thinking of them as a girl was definitely better than a stupid boy thinking of them as a boy, even if it was only the stupid opinion of a stupid boy.

Okay, you probably don't know why Tabby was so angry at me, which makes sense seeing as it happened before this story started. You see, last week I decided to start thinking of Tabby as a boy. But not to make fun of her. I have trouble talking to girls, so this was like an experiment.

It was working too. It was definitely easier to talk to her. At least, it was until she found out I was doing it.

That happened in class. We had to split up into boys and girls, and before I was thinking straight, I waved Tabby over to the boys' side.

'Boys on this side, Tabs!'

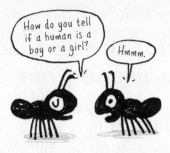

She was really
embarrassed by that,
in front of everyone.
Scabs tried to fix it by
saying, 'Don't worry Tabby, Freddy just thinks
you're a boy, he said so.'

Great. Thanks Scabs, but in the future, I might do
my own fixing.

Ever since then, Tabby has been getting angrier
and angrier. This was even after I told her that
she could be a girl again.

I thought saying that would smooth everything
over, but it didn't help at all.

She said, 'Oh, thanks so much, Freddy, gosh, you
mean that I can be a girl again? Did you hear that,
girls? I can be a girl again. That's such a relief,
like ...

'Who cares what you think, anyway!!?'

I told her I was sorry, and I was! I felt really bad. Well, to tell the truth, I was feeling more worried than bad. Her birthday party was coming up and I was worried she wouldn't invite me.

And I know that sounds a bit selfish, like I'm being unfeeling of her feelings, but she does get angry quite a lot and she does only have one birthday party a year. And, the whole town was going to get invited, so I would be the only one not going. Like, the party invitation would look like this ...

To Everyone (except FREDDY)

You are all invited to my PARTY in the park. I can't wait! yAy!!! PARTY TIME!!! See you all there! (except FREDDY).

Anyway, all of that was in the past because I did get invited to Tabby's party AND it's going to be awesome!

They're having it in the park because she has so many cousins and uncles and aunts that when they're all together you can't fit them into one house.

Your name Freddy?

Nah.

Looks like we're invited to a party!

And, they're having a jumping castle for little kids and a mechanical bull ride for bigger kids.

That's right, a mechanical bull!

I can't wait to have a go.

What you do is, you sit on it, hold a piece of rope and then hang on as it starts to move up and down and sideways like a real bull trying to throw you off.

I'm actually the best bull-rider in town. By far, yeah ... or like, I'm pretty sure I am.

I haven't actually ever ridden one before ... but when I think about riding one, like when I imagine myself riding a bull, I never fall off and I'm by far way better than anyone else.

There's a prize for the best rider too. It's called the Buckaroo Blue, whatever that is. I'll beat my friends for sure.

Talking of friends, my best friend Blocker was given the job of looking after a new kid at school. His name was Hugo.

Blocker had to show him around the school and hang with him in the playground so he wouldn't get lonely or sad. That meant Hugo was hanging out with me and our friends.

At lunchtime, Hugo told us that he was from a country called Hungary, which made him Hungarian, which we all thought was pretty funny as we were Hungry too, it being lunchtime.

After we'd eaten our lunches, Scabs said he was no longer from Hungry but was now from a place called Fairly Full and if he had the chocolate milk he was planning on having then he would be from the land of Totally Stuffed.

Blocker said he wanted to visit that country too, and was planning to buy a sausage roll to get there.

'So what's it like to come from a country that's always hungry?' Scabs asked.

Tabby pulled me away from the others. My heart started beating faster. It always did when we talked, just the two of us. I never knew what to say.

'Freddy, you still haven't told me. Why did you think of me as a boy? I thought we liked each other.'

My head turned down. 'I don't know, just being stupid I guess.'

My answer was the stupid thing. I couldn't talk to girls like this and especially Tabby, about whether I liked her.

It really embarrassed me.

'I didn't mean for you to know I was doing it. Scabs just went and said it.'

'But all the boys seemed to know about it.'

'Yeah, I told them. Sorry.'

I had no trouble talking to boys!

'So did you do it because I look like a boy?'

'No!' My head leapt up. 'Not at all, you're, ahh ...'

I needed to escape. I turned away. 'Hey Block! Don't eat all that sausage roll yourself. I want to visit Totally Stuffed too.'

I left her there.

'What about you, Coop, you want to go to Totally Stuffed?'

Cooper laughed, 'Yeah, I hate Hungry. Hungry sucks.'

'YOU CAN'T SAY THAT!'

We all spun around. Hugo's face was bright red.

'You people! Hungary is a great country and you laugh at it? And now you say you hate it!' He pointed fiercely at Cooper. 'Well, I hate you!'

'It's a joke,' said Blocker, putting a hand on Hugo's shoulder. 'Just a joke!'

Hugo brushed the hand off. 'You cannot joke about my country! You know nothing! My people are great, better than you!'

He was pointing at Cooper again, who threw his hands up and said, 'Whatever you think, man.' Cooper was cool that way. 'Sorry about ... whatever I said.'

Blocker led Hugo away and I went with them. Everyone else was looking at each other in shock, some hiding smiles.

'Hey, Hugo,' I said. 'Why don't you come over to my place after school? Block can come too. We'll hang out.'

Hugo sulkily agreed.

Mum was real pleased that I brought the new kid home. Or she was for a while.

Until she noticed ...

Like I'd noticed too.

I'd seen him doing it at school but I didn't think much about it because Hugo was new and he was nervous and heaps of people do it sometimes.

But MUM! I could see that she was going to say something for sure, so I grabbed Hugo and took him to the TV before she did. And I knew exactly what she was going to say too, because she used to say it to me ...

'Get your finger out of your nose!

'Where are you going to put that lump of disgusting mess, now that it's on your finger?

I wish I had a nose

I wish I had a finger

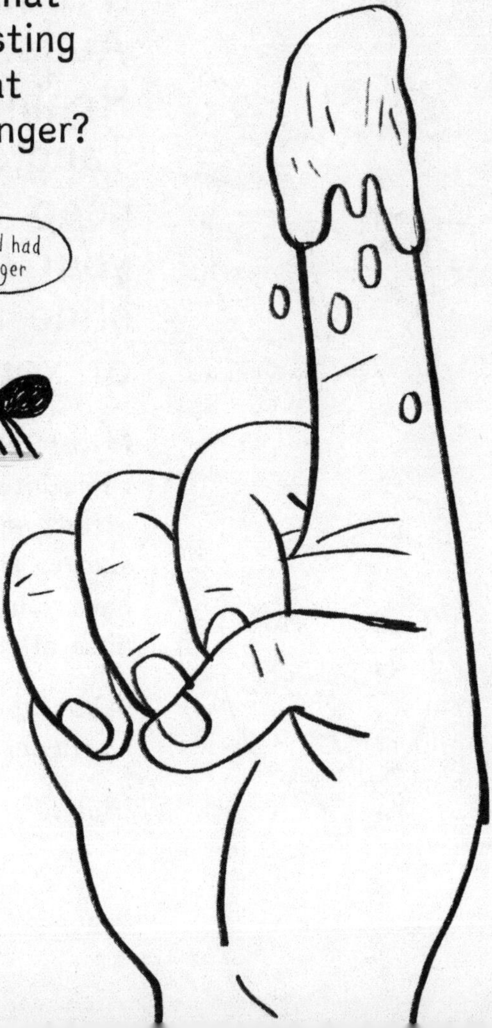

'Did you just eat that?

'Stop that! Save some room for dinner!

'Frederick Augustus Reginald Tangles, if you keep that up your brain will slide right out of your nose!'

My little sister, Jessica, came into the TV room and after a minute or so she said to Hugo, 'Why do you have your finger up your nose all the time?'

'I don't,' said Hugo, taking his finger out of his nose.

'But ...'

'Just watch TV!' I cried.

As soon as Jessica stopped looking he put his finger back in his nose, wiggled it around and then put it in his mouth!

Jessica kept looking over at him and I knew she was about to say, your finger is in your nose again, because it was!

I grabbed Hugo again and took him outside, away from my family.

'Let's play catch,' I said.

'But I wanted to watch TV!' Hugo wasn't happy and I understood. No-one likes to be disturbed halfway through eating.

Blocker turned up and the three of us played catch but Hugo was dropping the ball on purpose and eventually yelled, 'If you're not going to let me watch TV, I'm going home!'

And off he stormed.

I said to Blocker, 'He seems to get angry a lot.'

Block shrugged. 'Maybe, but the storm never lasts. The sun must come out eventually.'

Good old Blocker was always positive. 'Russian saying?' I asked. Blocker was Russian and loved his sayings.

Blocker nodded. 'Hugo just needs time to get used to us. I will help him. Russians and Hungarians are not so different. We are like brothers.'

After Blocker left, Mum called me over as I came into the house. She was changing a light globe and asked me to go up the stepladder to plug it in.

I kept walking. 'Sorry Mum, too much homework.'

'But it will only take a minute!'

I went straight to my room, closed the door and threw myself on my bed. I had just lied to my mother! And so easily! But what choice did I have? Nobody could ever know my secret. Not even Mum! She could never know, no-one could ever know ... that I'm afraid of heights. Really, really, badly, afraid of heights. No way could I go up a stepladder.

One time I even fainted when I looked up at a tall building. It went all swirly and before I knew it I was waking up from the ground with Blocker looking down at my face.

I pretended that I felt tired and decided to have a sleep. Blocker thought that was a pretty weird thing to do on a footpath in the middle of the city where people had to like, walk around me, but at least he didn't know the truth.

Even when we're in the park and my friends climb a tree, I never follow them. I just pretend I'm doing something more fun.

As I lay on my bed, I started to think about Tabby's party and how much fun it would be. How I was going to be the champion rider, and win the Buckaroo Blue.

When suddenly it hit me: a great idea!

Well, I think it was. The problem is, I've had great ideas in the past and they haven't always worked out. Like the great idea was actually a bad idea.

In fact, before I tell you about my great idea for Tabby's birthday party, I should tell you about other times I've had great ideas.

These are my three worst:
• Washing the dog
• Helping an old lady across the street
• Giving someone some money.

First, washing the dog.

Mince stank!

I don't know if you've ever had a dog, but I do and if there's one thing I've learned, it's that dogs like to roll in dirty things. Mince likes to roll in other dogs' poo.

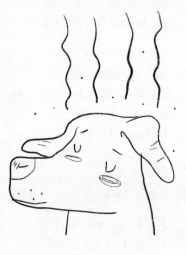

Could you imagine doing that?

Your friend does a poo on the grass and instead of telling them how disgusting they are you go over to it, sniff it, lick it, eat some and then roll in it!

That's what Mince does.

And it's not like he thinks *Oops, I shouldn't have eaten that,* because he's done it so many times now he should have realised. The problem is he actually really likes the taste of it!

And then of course he rolls in what is left.

He actually rolls in it to smell nice, like Mum puts on perfume ... except Mince puts on poo.

And like, maybe if the other dogs ran away from Mince then Mince might stop doing it, but they don't. They think it's a good idea.

Anyway, Mince rolled in poo after sniffing it and licking it and he really stank.

When we got home Mum ordered him straight outside to be hosed down. I was about to hose him when Jessica said we should give him a proper bath. That sounded like fun, so the two of us put Mince in a big bucket of soapy water and washed him real nice and it was fun and I think even Mince liked it.

When it was time to wash
the suds off, I got the hose,
which was on one of those
wind-up rollers. Jessica
turned the tap on and I
had the hose nozzle on
closed so water couldn't
come out until I was ready.

Only, the water did come out because the nozzle
blew off the hose! And the hose was like, flashing
around like a crazy snake because no-one was
holding it. Mince freaked! He bit the hose so hard
his tooth got stuck in
it which made the
water blast into
his face and his
mouth. He just
took off, straight
inside the kitchen
door with the
hose still stuck
to his tooth and
unravelling off
the reel!

I chased
after him,
right through the
kitchen and into the lounge room
with water spraying everywhere.

When I finally caught him I had to wrestle him to get the hose off.

Mum turned up just after I got the hose off Mince's tooth and this is what she saw ...

That's right. It looked like me and Mince were happily playing in the lounge room with the hose on full bore!!!

She was so mad.

Everything was so wet my parents had to turn off the electricity to the whole house, pull up the carpet and take the couches outside for drying.

Boy, did I get into trouble that day.

Dad said I shouldn't have run in after Mince. I could have just turned the hose off at the tap.

Anyway, then there was the time I tried to help an old lady across the street.

HELPING OLD LADIES BADGE

And yes, I know, helping an old lady across the street is about the best thing you can ever do. In Scouts they give you a badge or something for it.

My dad even has a saying for when he does something that's good but not really that good. He says, 'Thanks, but it's not like I helped an old lady across the street.' So it really must be one of the best things you can ever do.

So there was this old lady who looked like she needed help.

I asked her and she said, 'Oh, how sweet of you, young man. My eyes aren't what they used to be. Are there any cars coming?'

I looked up the street and said, 'No,' and shook my head too because I could tell that her ears weren't what they used to be either.

Then I added, 'But there is a pushbike coming so we'll wait for that.'

Road clear?

As far as I can see

Only she didn't hear me say that because her ears weren't what they used to be. She only saw me shake my head.

She stepped straight out onto the road, right in front of that pushbike which was coming fast down the hill.

It was all my fault.

The bike rider slammed on his brakes but it was way too late and all I could think to do to stop the old lady from getting smashed was to jump in front of the bike ... which I did.

And got totally smashed!

The bike slammed straight into me. I was crunched so bad that I think I might have even fainted for a second, because I woke up on the ground.

I started groaning and trying to move. Everything hurt, but I knew I had done the right thing because I'd saved the old lady. I was a hero. I imagined how the newspapers and the television were going to interview me and ask me

what it felt like to be so brave.

Only I didn't get a medal or even a thank you. When the bike smashed into me, it pushed me into the old lady and I knocked her handbag out of her hand.

So there I was, lying on the ground, all dizzy and hurting and bleeding, when the old lady started whacking me with her walking stick.

She thought I was trying to steal her bag because it was lying on the ground with me.

She hit me really hard three times before I could crawl away.

She called me a *rapscallion*.

Like, I don't know what a *rapscallion* is, but I'm pretty sure it doesn't mean a nice person who washes dogs or throws themselves in front of bikes to save old ladies. I'm also pretty sure it doesn't mean someone who gives money to people in need, which is number three on my list.

I gave a kid some money to buy a chocolate bar.

That's all I did!

A bunch of us heard about a new chocolate bar, called a Bonzabar, so after school we went to the shops to buy one. We all bought one but one kid didn't have enough money so I gave it to him. How could that be wrong?

Every bar of chocolate came with a Bonzabar Hero Card inside. What you do is, you battle other kids against their cards and whoever wins the battle gets a piece of the other person's chocolate.

It was pretty cool and we're all there with our chocolate and cards. The kid I gave the money to said, 'Thanks, Freddy,' as he took his first bite.

Well, that was the last thing he said for a while.

A couple of seconds later, his face turned red and puffy and then he started wheezing and everything went crazy after that with adults running everywhere, an ambulance arriving, parents crying ...

He ended up okay ... apparently he was allergic to peanuts.

Peanuts!

He didn't know the Bonzabar had peanuts in it and when his parents started asking how he got the chocolate bar everyone pointed at me.

Well, I've got to say that I felt totally ratted on.

His parents gave me a pretty mean stare, I can tell you, and they told my parents that I nearly killed their son.

So as you can see, you have to be careful about coming up with great ideas because they can turn you into a bag-stealing chocolate-bar murderer who likes to turn lounge rooms into swimming pools.

So anyway, I had this great idea for Tabby's birthday and I was sure this time it wouldn't end in disaster. How could it? All I'd be doing is dressing up like a cowboy for when I rode the mechanical bull.

It was him.

I would make it secret, like I'd go in my normal clothes and then just before I rode, I'd put on my cowboy clothes. I'd look like a real cowboy, and Tabby would be impressed ...

Hmmm, that was strange ... I wanted to impress her ...

I'd never really cared about impressing Tabby before. Like, I was always happy that she liked me and that she was my friend but I wanted her to think I was like ... the best boy she knows.

Wearing my cowboy gear would impress her for sure. I'd be the best and most awesome-looking cowboy this town has ever known!

Jessica came into my room, I mean our room.

'You don't look like you're doing homework.'

'I'm thinking.'

'What are you thinking about?'

'I'm thinking about how much I want my own room.'

'Not until I can read. That's what Dad said.'

That was true. We have a spare room that's small and dark and full of junk, but I'll take it!

'Are you going to read to me tonight, Freddy?'

'Are you going to play a joke on me tomorrow?'

'No.'

'Then I'll read to you.'

Jessica was still playing jokes on me. I'm a deep sleeper. I don't wake up easily and Jessica kept doing things.

The other day she joined my eyebrows together with a permanent marker.

Last week she put shaving cream on one of my hands and then tickled my nose with a feather so I whacked the cream into my face.

I'm reading to her so she learns to read faster and I can get my own room. I actually don't mind reading to her anyway. I usually read nursery rhymes because she likes them and they're easy to read and they've got good pictures. But boy, are they nasty!

Nursery rhymes are supposed to be for little kids to put them to sleep, but like, listen to this ...

Little Polly Flinders
Sat among the cinders,
Warming her pretty little toes.
Mother came and caught her,
And whipped her little daughter
For spoiling her nice new clothes.

Can you believe it? Little Polly got her clothes a bit dirty so her mum whipped her!

WHIPPED!

Why do people even wear clothes?

No idea.

Then there's Goosey, Goosey Gander. Like, I don't even know what a Goosey, Goosey Gander is but if you ever hear someone say *Goosey, Goosey Gander* then start saying your prayers ...

Goosey, Goosey Gander, where shall I wander?
Upstairs, downstairs and in my lady's chamber.
There I met an old man who wouldn't say his prayers.
I took him by the left leg and threw him down the stairs.

SO, little kiddies, just before you go to sleep, I'm going to read you a lovely soothing nursery rhyme about some crazy person wandering around a house saying Goosey, Goosey Gander and chucking people down stairs!

BY THE LEG!

That should get you sweetly off to la la land.

Yeah, right.

And that's not the worst one, either.

No, the worst one is called Little Miss Muffet. I always try to miss the page that has Little Miss Muffet on it but sometimes Jessica remembers and makes me read it to her ...

Little Miss Muffet sat on a tuffet,
Eating her curds and whey.
Along came a spider,
Who sat down beside her
And frightened Miss Muffet away.

I know, nothing really bad happens in this one, but it's about spiders and I so hate spiders. Even the picture of the spider in the book freaks me out!

I hate spiders and I can't tell Jessica because I know what will happen. I'll wake up one morning with a dead spider on my face!

Jessica even came up with her own Little Miss Muffet poem because she said the poem sounded stupid. Like, what is a *tuffet* and what is *curds and whey*? It sounds totally disgusting, like something no-one would ever eat, so Jessica's poem goes ...

Little Miss Clare sat on a chair,
Eating her toast and jam.
Along came a spider
Who sat down beside her
And Miss Clare with
her shoe went WHAM!

I like Jessica's poem better because the spider is WHAMMED, only it still freaks me out that Jessica thinks she can actually get close enough to a spider to WHAM it. No way could I do that. I have to stay as far away from them as I can because they are like, tiny monsters.

Have you ever seen a spider up close? They have black beady eyes, creepy legs that are hairy all over and pincers for biting.

What's even worse, we actually have spiders like that inside our house.

And do you know what they're called?

Huntsman spiders. Yeah. And do you know why they're called huntsman spiders? Because they hunt!

I've seen them. I've even seen one with really long hairy legs right above my bed at night, just looking at me, daring me to go to sleep so it can start hunting. And what does a huntsman hunt? It hunts MAN.

It's not called a Huntsbugs spider or even
a Friendly to Freddy spider. No. It's called a
huntsman spider because it hunts man, and it
does it with really big pincers and long hairy legs.

How can you possibly go to sleep with that
monster on the loose?

And when I do finally fall asleep, sometimes
I dream about them hunting me!

And they're huge, and I can't ever run fast enough to get away. Like, I know I can run faster but I'm stuck in this weird slow motion, which makes it impossible for me to escape no matter how hard I try. I go nowhere and I wake up sweating all over.

BUT that's not the scariest dream I have. My scariest dreams don't have anything to do with spiders at all.

Believe it or not, there is something even scarier than giant hairy spider monsters trying to kill me ... and I dream about it way too often.

It's me being naked. Yeah, naked in front of strangers!

Or at school!

Now that's a nightmare: naked at school in front of everyone.

And do you know why I'm naked in my dreams?

Because I forget to wear clothes!

I forget to put them on! How stupid is that?

And then I hope that nobody notices.

As if nobody would!!!

And that's the crazy thing ... they *don't* notice. Somehow, they don't notice.

They just carry on like normal, only I'm totally torn up inside worrying that any moment they will see.

It's the worst nightmare anyone could possibly ever have!

It's worse than being hunted by a gruesome fang-infested monster.

I don't know anyone who likes being naked in front of other people ...actually, that's not quite right.

We don't go to the beach very often, but in summer when it's hot, Dad rings up his brother, my Uncle Reggie, and off we go.

Uncle Reggie has three kids. They're my cousins, and they live near the beach so they're really good in the waves. All I can do in the surf is get smashed, but it's still heaps of fun.

Anyway, when we leave the beach, Dad won't let me in the car without a shower. He says, 'Freddy, you've got half the beach in those shorts of yours.'

I don't sleep either but I still have a dream ... that humans will one day show us ants some respect!

Like that kid down there?

Which is true. After being dumped all day long, I have sand in every little crack and crevice where sand can possibly go. But that doesn't mean I want a shower at the beach. I'd rather be dumped by a hundred-foot wave!

If Tabby asked what I'd rather do, take a shower at the beach or have so much sand in my shorts I got a big rash between my legs, then I'd say, **bring on the rash.**

It might hurt like chunks to walk for a few days, but anything is better than showering in the surf club, because everyone can see everyone else!

My cousins don't seem to mind. They all shower together like one big happy family, only I don't think showering together is any way to make a family happy. That's what computers are for.

That's rude ... we can't help walking with our legs apart.

No respect!

All the boys and all the men from the whole beach shower together!

Naked!

Together!

And the big hairy men in there don't even care about the hair all over them. They even talk to each other as if they're not naked, as if they just met in the street and stopped for a chat.

It's mad!

And then, there are really old men with saggy skin and little kids who wee on the floor where we all stand.

I get into a corner so no-one can see my doodle.

Like, there's nothing wrong with my doodle, I just don't want anyone else seeing it. Mum's alright, and Dad, and even Jessica, but I like to limit the number of people who have seen my doodle to just a few people. I think three is enough.

Luckily, I'm pretty sure it's been proven by doctors that the only thing that can make someone feel better after a naked nightmare in a surf club shower is an ice cream.

Dad usually comes through with that.

So anyway, I was on the bus to school when Hugo sat down next to me and said, 'You should have let me watch TV yesterday. I wanted to watch TV.'

'Oh right,' I said, not sure if he was joking or not. 'My sister was annoying,' I added, looking for a clue.

'When my sister gets annoying, I punch her,' said Hugo.

I still wasn't sure if he was joking. 'Well, punching sisters can be very satisfying,' I said, making it clear I was joking.

He just stared at me. 'What are you doing?'

'Nothing.'

I was actually checking to see that I remembered to wear clothes.

A bit later on we were waiting for the morning bell, playing handball, when Hugo said to everyone, 'I went to Freddy's house yesterday.'

It was hardly news. Blocker suggested we do it again today, after school. Cooper and Scabs said they would come over too.

Hugo said, 'Why don't we go to someone else's house? Freddy's house is too boring.'

Boring?

'Boring?' asked Scabs.

'Yeah, his mum kept staring at me and his little sister is annoying and Freddy didn't let me watch my favourite show on TV.'

What? Like, what?

'His mum was staring?' asked Cooper.

'Yeah, it was really weird.'

Who did Hugo think he was? Here he was, the new kid with his finger up his nose, eating his snot like it was chocolate, and he thinks we're weird?

I was annoyed.

'Yeah, well, maybe if you weren't picking your nose and eating it all the time my mum wouldn't have been staring at you and my sister wouldn't have had to ask why you do it and we could have watched TV.'

Everyone just looked at me.

'WELL, HE DOES! He spent the whole time with his finger up his nose and eating it. He does it all the time! Haven't you seen him?'

No-one said anything.

Hugo's face turned bright red.

It was awkward. I decided to say something funny, to lighten the mood. I wiggled my fingers at them all and said, 'Maybe he does it because he's Super Booger Boy!'

Cooper wiggled his fingers at Scabs and cried out, 'Hey yeah. Look out, Scabs, or I'll get you with my booger fingers!'

That was better!

Scabs started going, 'No, no, keep them away from me!'

We started chasing each other. I went after Tabby but she didn't move. At least her legs didn't. Her mouth was moving fast.

'Remember when you were called Fartboy and everyone was chasing everyone with Fartboy Fever? Remember how that felt?'

So? And then I realised. Tabby was right. This looked exactly the same: chasing each other with booger fingers.

I called out, 'STOP!'

Blocker was already pulling at Cooper to stop.

Hugo ran off and Blocker went after him, growling as he passed me, 'Good one, Freddy!'

Everyone was awkward again.

I said to everyone, 'But he really does eat his snot.'

Tabby frowned. 'It's still no reason to bully him.'

'Bully? Me? I'm not a bully. I wasn't!'

'So calling the new kid Super Booger Boy isn't bullying?'

'I was just joking!'

'I suppose he did say something mean about your family.'

'Yeah!'

'So you had to get him back, I suppose.'

'Yeah. I did!'

'So you intentionally embarrassed the new kid in front of everyone because he annoyed you?'

'Y ... ahhh!'

I always remember too late that I should never argue with Tabby. I never win.

'Okay, alright! I shouldn't have said it. Happy now?'

I never found out if she was happy now because the School Captain, Ambrose Graham, came over and said I had to go see Deputy Principal Mulcaster because I had been reported for bullying!

'But I wasn't,' I said to him. 'I was just joking ...'

Ambrose didn't care. I had to go see Mr Mulcaster.

Mr Mulcaster is the scariest teacher in the school. And not because he's the Deputy Principal who yells at us for not lining up in canteen, or talking in assembly, or running in the halls, or sometimes for something that we didn't even know was a rule. No, he's scary because he has a glass eye!

One of his real eyes is missing, so in the hole where his eye should be is this round piece of glass that looks like an eye.

He doesn't actually take it out, but he could if he wanted.

Mr Mulcaster says he lost it in a car accident. I'm not so sure. He's always going on about maths. He says that when he was a student, he used to do an hour

of maths homework every
night and that's why he's
so good at it. I think he
lost his eye then. I think his
eye got so bored, it decided
to leave and go find a more
interesting head.

that's it I'm
outta here!

Having a glass eye makes
Mr Mulcaster look totally freaky because the
glass eye never looks the same way as his good eye.

Whenever he is in our
classroom it looks like he can
see the whole room at once.
Like, he can be talking
to a kid on one side
of the room and his
glass eye will point
right across to the
other side as if he's
watching everyone
else.

So there I was, in front of Mr Mulcaster, and he
was staring down at me with one eye while the
other one was pointed out the window like he was
also on playground duty.

'No-one likes a bully, Freddy,' he started and I
had to agree. I hated them too. Sid Malone was
still fresh in my memory.

'You made a new student feel very sad and alone today, Freddy. He's frightened and he tells me you've turned all of your friends against him.'

That wasn't right.

'No sir, I didn't. My friends think I did the wrong thing. They still like Hugo.'

Mr Mulcaster's eyebrows lifted. 'So you agree that you did the wrong thing.'

'I ... I ... no ... well ... maybe I went too far.'

'Freddy, I've called your mother to the school and you need to understand that we have a strict policy of no bullying. This sort of behaviour usually results in suspension from school.'

'My mother, sir?'

He kept talking after he said my mother was coming, but I didn't hear it. All I heard was the noise inside my head ...

Mr Mulcaster might have yelled, TIGER! Run for your life! And I wouldn't have moved because I wouldn't have heard him.

Mum walked in and her face said it all.

Mr Mulcaster told her how I was guilty of bullying. Mum's face went redder and redder with every word.

'Well, I'm very surprised and disappointed, Mr Mulcaster,' started my mum. 'Freddy knows how cruel bullying is. He has been the victim of a bully himself. I can assure you that Freddy is going to be in a lot of trouble when he gets home.'

Mum looked down at me, with all the parts of her face promising punishments.

Her hand looked pretty angry as well.

'Tell me, Mr Mulcaster, what did Freddy do to the poor child?'

'Ah, I've written it down, here let me see.'

Mr Mulcaster squinted at a sheet of paper. 'Your son said in front of a large crowd that the boy Hugo is always picking his nose and eating it. Freddy then suggested that Hugo might be Super Booger Boy.'

Mum slowly turned to me.

'Is that what you said?'

I nodded, feeling about as small as an ant.

Mum turned back to Mr Mulcaster.

'Freddy's exactly right, Mr Mulcaster. Hugo was at our house yesterday afternoon and he was picking his nose and eating it all the time! Quite disgusting! Though at least he did know what he wanted to do with it, Mr Mulcaster. Most people pick their nose without ever thinking what they'll do with that slimy little package. Stuck with it then, aren't they? Rub it under a table or into the carpet, but not Hugo, that boy has quite the appetite.'

Go Mum!

For a moment I think both of Mr Mulcaster's eyes actually looked in the same direction, as if even his glass eye was surprised at Mum's words.

'Yes, but err, that's not the point, Mrs Tangles. Freddy made Hugo sad.'

Mum's eyebrows raised high.

'Sad? What's wrong with a little truth, Mr Mulcaster? Hugo picks his nose so much I wouldn't be surprised if his brain slides right out of his nose. I think my son has done Hugo a huge favour. What boy wants to go through life without a brain?'

Not me! And even though Mr Mulcaster didn't answer Mum's question, I think he likes having one too.

I suppose he can play computers!

can I blink now?

actually it's really hard to keep an eyebrow up like this for a long time anyway

I'm still watching you

nothing wrong with being a little CHEEKY I suppose...

brussel sprouts aren't actually that bad tasting

yes they are!

That was about it. All of the parts of Mum's face that were promising punishments went back to normal, sort of ...

See ya.

Oh ... okay, well just forget what I said earlier about stomping— I didn't mean that.

Mr Mulcaster sent me back to class. I wasn't suspended. He just mumbled something about apologising to Hugo and to watch my behaviour in the future.

I didn't mind apologising. I was in the wrong. He was the new kid, and I could have laughed it off.

My teacher, Mr Brody, pretty much said the same thing, at least I think he did. He uses weird words sometimes. When I came back to class he talked to me quietly about how should apologise and at the end he said, 'And remember, Freddy, nobody likes a snollygoster.'

I nodded in total agreement. No way did I want to be known as a snollygoster ... whatever that was! It sounded bad, kind of snotty like a snot ball or snotty spit.

Then he said, 'Okay, Freddy, back to your seat, lickety-split.'

Lickety-split?

That was kind of like spit too, like licking spit!

Those are the kind of weird words he uses but what was even weirder than those words was that they were actually in the dictionary!

I looked them up. Lickety-split meant right away or fast, and snollygoster: there it was, sitting in the dictionary like a proper word. It meant someone not to be trusted.

At recess I told Hugo I was sorry.

I said it right in front of everyone. When I was finished, Tabby came over, grabbed my hand and gave it a squeeze like she was proud of me. 'That was so cool.'

What wasn't cool was Hugo.

He said my apology meant nothing.

I thought it meant a lot. I mean, I really meant it when I said it.

He said that in Hungary they have a saying.

A saying! Just like Blocker!

'The chicken will not fly into your mouth.'

I had no idea what that meant, only I knew for sure I didn't want a chicken flying into my mouth.

It sounded so stupid I sort of laughed at it and so did some of the others, but that only made Hugo angrier.

He said the only way the insult against him could be fixed was by a challenge.

Blocker said, 'Yeah, that's how they do things where we come from.'

Where we come from?

I thought Blocker came from the house across the road from my house.

A challenge ...

'Okay,' I said, looking around. 'What about rock-chucking? First one to hit that pole over there is the winner.'

He said, 'That is no test to decide who is the better man.'

The better man?

The challenge was: at Tabby's party, whoever could stay on the mechanical bull for the longest time would be the winner.

I couldn't believe it. What an idiot! Didn't he know that I was the best rider in the whole town?

Then he said again, 'And remember this, Freddy Tangles, the chicken will not fly into your mouth.'

I said good, because that was a really weird thing Hugo was saying about chickens. Then I said, 'And no chicken is going to beat me on the mechanical bull, because I'm the best rider in town. And if you don't want to accept my apology then why don't you go find some other friends.'

Blocker edged over to Hugo. 'You already have one friend, Hugo. Let's go.'

That shocked me. 'Block, what are you doing?'

'Looking after Hugo. What are you doing?'

I was watching my best friend take Hugo's side!

'But ...'

As they left together, Blocker turned back and said, 'Remember this, Freddy, a hungry pig dreams of acorns, but it's only a dream.'

Chickens? Pigs? Acorns? Hugo and Blocker were just like each other.

Hugo nodded as if what Blocker said made sense, but the only thing I understood was that my best friend was walking off with Hugo.

As they walked away I saw Blocker put his hand on Hugo's shoulder and then they went around the corner and that was it, my best friend was gone.

Tabby filled the silence left by Blocker leaving. 'What would you prefer to do, go to a birthday party or ride on a mechanical bull?'

No-one was in the mood for one of Tabby's questions, but we all answered anyway because it was a tradition. Everyone else preferred the party because parties go for longer and have excellent food, where the mechanical bull is just a quick ride. I said I'd prefer the mechanical

Are you following me because I'm your best friend?

I'm following you because you're leaving a smell that MAKES me follow you to find food for the nest.

I'll take that as a yes.

bull because I was going to beat Hugo on it.

I asked Tabby what Hugo and Blocker's sayings meant.

'Hugo was saying that you can't just say you're the best at riding the mechanical bull.'

'How did you get that from chickens flying into my mouth?'

'Because you have to catch the chicken before you can eat it. It won't just fly into your mouth.'

Cooper grabbed a chicken sandwich from his lunchbox and cried, 'Look out! This chicken is flying into my mouth!'

He chucked a triangle of sandwich at his mouth. Most of it bounced off his face and fell on the ground.

'Nuts!'

Tabby laughed. 'And some people can't even get chicken into their mouth when it's safely in a sandwich.'

She turned back to me.

'But Freddy, the saying means you have to practise, it won't just happen. It's pretty much the same as Blocker's saying. You can dream about riding the mechanical bull really well, but it's just a dream.'

'But I can! I can ride it for as long as I want.'

Tabby looked at me for a good long second.
'Everyone gets thrown off.'

Tabby sounded like she knew what she was talking about.

'Okay, but all I have to do is beat Hugo. I have to. You heard him. That stuff about the better man. It's me or him. It's all that matters!'

'All that matters?' Tabby asked, sounding strange.

'Yes. I really can beat him.'

'I don't care!'

That caught me by surprise. Tabby's cheeks were turning red and I thought she might be about to cry.

'It's my party and all you care about is this stupid challenge! You care more about riding the bull than you do about my birthday!'

'No I don't.'

'Yes you do!'

Her voice went quiet. 'You said so, when I asked which one you would prefer. You said, riding the bull, not my birthday ...'

'Oh ...'

'You think it's all that matters.'

Then she started crying.

Tabby stood there crying right in front of me. Tears were streaming down her face and ... I'm not really sure what happened after that. I was standing there in front of her and then she wasn't there, no one was there, just a few blurry shapes and some bouncing up and down.

And then I realised I was running.

I had run away!

I don't remember making that decision, but it did seem like a good decision because there wasn't a girl crying in front of me anymore.

Back in class, I had Blocker on one side of the room, ignoring me with his new best friend, Hugo, and Tabby on the other side, staring at me with red, tear-stained eyes.

'We need to move into groups,' said Mr Brody. No-one moved much because it was after lunch. 'Come on kids, no lollygagging.'

We all looked around the room for someone gagging on a lolly. We didn't see anyone.

Mr Brody realised we had no idea what he was talking about. 'Kids, lollygagging means not doing anything. Don't you kids read the dictionary?'

Mr Brody actually does read the dictionary.

'Sorry sir,' said Cooper. 'Must have skipped that word.'

I joined with Tabby, hoping to make it up to her. 'What do you think he's going to get us to do?' I asked.

Tabby didn't say anything.

Hugo came over and said, 'Tabby, why don't you come join us? We won't run away.'

Tabby got up and left without a word.

Hugo said to her, 'I wish we had girls as pretty as you in Hungary.'

She smiled and blushed. Hugo smirked down at me as he left.

After school I went over to Block's house to talk to him but he wasn't there. His mum said he was over at Hugo's.

Over at Hugo's!

And his mum said, 'Isn't Hugo a lovely boy? He's coming over for dinner tonight.'

I couldn't believe it. I used to be the friend invited over to Blocker's for dinner and now it was Hugo.

I was sitting out in the gutter, thinking about my ex-best friend, when Cooper rode past. He was going to the park so I went with him.

'I heard Hugo calling Tabby pretty in class this arvo,' said Cooper.

'Yeah.'

'I thought she was like, with you.'

'No way'

I always denied that sort of thing right away because it was embarrassing. But this was Cooper. He was cool and all the girls liked him. Nearly every lunchtime a girl came over to him and said, 'So-and-so wants to go around with you, will I say yes or no?'

Nearly every time Cooper goes 'sure, whatever', so I wasn't sure how many girlfriends he had at the moment and maybe he didn't know either.

If I couldn't talk to Cooper about girls then I couldn't talk to anyone. 'I think she's mad at me for running away from her, you know, when she was crying.'

'So why did you run away?'

'I don't know, I was scared.'

'Scared? Did you think at all?'

'No. I just ran.'

'Really? That's like spiders.'

'Spiders!' I exploded. 'Girls are like spiders?'

'No,' said Cooper, beginning to realise how much I knew about girls. 'You running away is like spiders. Girls aren't like spiders.'

'Oh ...'

That made sense, because I've never seen a girl crawling on my wall with huge hairy legs.

'No, I did an assignment on spiders. They've got this ... ummm, flight or fight instinct when they're in danger, and I think that's what happened to you.'

'Flight or fight?'

'Yeah, when there's danger you run away, or you stay and fight. It's only one or the other.'

'You know, I did feel in danger, like Tabby was crying and that was scary and I didn't know what to do. Like what can you say to a girl who's crying?'

'If you're scared, nothing. You can only fight or flight. Instinct. Like a spider.'

'Well, I didn't want to fight her, she was crying ... so I chose to run.'

'No, Freddy, you didn't choose. It was instinct. You didn't think, you just acted.'

'Yeah. Thanks, Cooper. Really then, she should be thanking me for running away.'

Girls were hard to work out. There I was, only able to run or fight, and she was angry at me for running!

'So did you see Hugo with Tabby in class? They were talking and laughing non-stop!'

Cooper nodded. 'I saw. And after school too. You think he's moving in on your girl?'

'She's not my girl ...'

Cooper was grinning.

'Well, we like each other you know, but it's not like we um, she um ...'

'Aha.'

'Shut up.'

Why was it so difficult?

'Cooper, how come so many girls like you?'

Cooper didn't have to think about that question.

'It's because I'm cool.'

Oh.

'What is cool, then?' I asked. 'Like how come you're so cool?'

'It's my hair.'

Cooper's hair is kind of long and blond.

'And my pool is cool.'

Everyone did want to swim in it.

'My bedroom is cool too, like it's huge and it's got a pinball machine in it.'

That was cool.

'And I say whatever all the time and that's cool.'

'You do say that a lot, and it is cool!'

'Whatever.

'That was cool.'

'I know.'

I wondered if I might be cool too. Like my hair isn't blond and I don't have a pool and I share a room with my little sister and I never say whatever but maybe I was cool too.

'Am I cool?'

Cooper looked at me like he was on this planet called Cool and he could barely see me on my faraway planet called Not Very Cool At All.

'So is it cool being cool?' I asked.

'It's cool, but sometimes it can be lonely.'

Scabs turned up and we started talking about the challenge that Hugo had made and we all agreed that I would win, but seeing what they said about chickens, pigs and acorns, we decided it would be a good idea if I did some practice.

The first thing we tried was the seesaw in the playground. I didn't want to get on. I'm afraid of heights, but I couldn't see a way out so I did. I sat at one end while Scabs and Cooper grabbed the other end and bounced it up and down, trying to get me to fall off.

I was so glad when they stopped. I jumped straight off.

'Well, that's enough practice for today.'

'No way,' said Scabs. 'We need to make sure you're ready.' He pointed to a branch in a tree above us. 'Climb up there and we'll bounce the branch.'

No chance. Never in a tree, ever! I had to come up with something quick, so I said, 'No, I'm doing Mulgarrie's Hill.'

That's a steep hill in the park where kids ride billycarts. Cooper and Scabs laughed at me. We ride our bikes on it all the time and even though it's a little bit steep it's easy to ride.

They were right. I was sounding lame, like I might be afraid of heights, so I said, 'No, I mean the bushy bit, not the grassy bit.'

They both said 'No way' at exactly the same time.

Next to the grass is a steep bit of trees and rocks that we climb through. No-one has ever ridden a bike down it. It's certain death. But even certain death was better than climbing onto a branch high up in a tree.

The hill was called Mulgarrie after a kid back in the dark ages, like way back even before computers existed. Apparently he was so annoyed that no one had invented computer games

yet that he climbed a tree on the hill and refused to come down until they were invented. Well, unfortunately lightning had already been invented by clouds, and the tree got blasted to bits and Mulgarrie was never seen again.

'You're crazy,' said Cooper, peering down through the trees from the top of the hill.

I was starting to think so too.

Scabs gushed, 'If you can make it down there, then no one can beat you. No way, not if you can do this!'

Scabs was right. If I could ride down this track, Hugo had no chance, and chickens and pigs and acorns beware.

This was my test. I stayed at the top of the hill while Cooper and Scabs rode around and down to the bottom. I peered down the path. It led down a steep track through

trees and onto rocks before a straight fall to
Scabs and Cooper.

'C'mon, Freddy! You can do it!'

I decided to start slow and if it was too hard, I
would stop.

Or so I thought!

As soon as I hit the steep bit, I put on my brakes,
but my bike just kept going, sliding on dirt and
leaves, straight into branches that slapped and
scratched my face and hands. I couldn't see
anything, and then I skidded onto the rocks. I was
bouncing, sliding,
leaning back and
hanging onto
my handlebars
while the
bike bucked
like a bull.

I could hear
Cooper and Scabs
screaming ...

I was totally out of control. Ahead was the last rock with nothing beyond it but air ... the big drop down to where Scabs and Cooper were.

I wanted off. This was too scary, too crazy. What was I thinking?! I wasn't going over that edge!

But it was getting closer. It was now or never. I had to jump off onto the rocks. Now! I had to do it now! And then it was too late. I hesitated, too afraid, and now ...

I was flying!

It was so peaceful.

It was like I had defeated the mechanical bull. I was the master! And nothing could throw Freddy Tangles ...

Except perhaps the ground.

Cooper and Scabs laughed and cheered and then went quiet, the kind of quiet you go after you realise the person you're laughing at actually hurt themselves.

Badly.

I landed on my shoulder. I lay there for a while because I couldn't move.

'Are you okay?' Cooper asked. 'That was awesome.'

I dragged myself up. My shoulder and neck wouldn't move and I was bleeding from heaps of scratches.

Scabs tried to make me feel better by saying that I had some really impressive scabs in the making ... as soon as I stopped bleeding.

Cooper was saying, 'You did it, Freddy. You rode it! No-one can beat you on that bull.'

I spat some dirt out of my mouth.

'I'm going home.' It was all I said, all I could say. I limped off.

'We'll look after your bike.'

I didn't say anything back. I could barely walk, let alone talk. I just needed to get home.

I was limping through the park when I saw Block and Hugo coming in my direction. I didn't want to be seen by them the way I was, so I crawled under a bush at the bottom of a tree.

They looked real chummy walking together.

'So the mechanical bull is going to be down here?' asked Hugo.

'Yeah. I've never seen one before. Does it look like a real bull?'

71

'Not really, but it moves like a bucking bull. You sit on it and hang on to a piece of rope and then they turn it on and speed it up.'

'Freddy doesn't know about you, does he? You'll beat him for sure.'

'You can't tell him.'

'I won't.'

'If you do I'll tell everyone you like Miranda Hume.'

'What? Why would you say that?'

'Hey, Tabby's coming. Don't say anything to her either. We'll make it a big surprise for everyone.'

Through the leaves I could see Tabby walking towards us. Whatever Hugo's secret was, it looked like I wasn't going to find out.

Hugo whispered, 'You know, I like Tabby. Do you think she would be my girlfriend?'

'Girlfriend?' Blocker said the word like he'd never said it before. 'Does she like you?'

'I'm going to ask her to be my girlfriend.'

'Wow! Can boys ask girls?'

'Why not?'

'I'm pretty sure the only way to get a girlfriend is wait in the playground until the friend of a girl you like comes over and asks.'

'Are you sure?'

'It's the only way I've ever seen it work, like I don't think a boy can ask until you ask a girl if she wants to get married or something.'

'Oh.' Hugo frowned at that. 'Well, if I tell her how much I like her, she will ask me for sure. Especially when I become the champion bull rider.'

'I think Tabby likes Freddy,' said Blocker.

'I know. That's why I will make her my girlfriend. Freddy will lose that too!'

I couldn't believe it.

Tabby arrived and Blocker said, 'Hi Tabby, what are you doing here?'

'My party is here on Saturday and I wanted to come and have a look. I'm looking for Freddy too, have you seen him?'

'Nah, not looking for him.'

That hurt.

Blocker went on, 'We were just talking about your party. It's going to be great. I can't wait.'

'Neither can I,' smiled Tabby.

'Neither can I,' said Hugo and Tabby beamed at him. Hugo purred, 'You are a very lovely person, Tabitha Henry. You deserve to have a wonderful birthday party with all of your friends and family and I am honoured to be coming.'

'Wow! Thank you Hugo.'

Hugo bowed, like a gentleman. 'In my country, we have a tradition where girls are escorted to their party by a boy of their choosing. I would be proud to escort you, Tabitha Henry, if you would permit me.'

'Oh, I, err.'

'It is not as a boyfriend, you understand, though that would be a great honour. Just someone to escort you to the party.'

'Um, okay then, an escort. If that's what you do in Hungary, that would be lovely.'

I don't know how I stayed quiet in that bush. I wanted to come out and rage at Hugo. I should have, but for what? For liking Tabby? For taking her away from me when she wasn't even my girlfriend because I was too afraid to ask? That was my problem; I was too afraid of everything! Of girls, of heights and spiders, and of jumping off bikes. I was a chicken, plain and simple, and I stayed in my bush like a chicken would.

Tabby left, looking back to smile and wave at Hugo.

'See,' said Hugo. 'I can make her my girlfriend.'

They left as well. I crawled out of the bush, hurting on the outside from my crash, and on the inside now too.

When I got home Mum thought I had been bashed by a bully.

'Who did this to you?'

When I told her I did it to myself she didn't believe me.

'No-one can hurt themselves that much.'

Well, they can if they ride down the bushy bit of Mulgarrie's Hill. But I didn't say that.

I said, 'I fell off my bike.'

Mum shook her head and spun me around, finding new scratches wherever she looked.

'How many times did you fall off your bike? A thousand?'

I did have lots of hurting and bleeding bits. Mum put me in a bath with salts and it felt amazing.

My shoulder and my neck loosened up. Mum came in later and said, 'I met Hugo's mum this afternoon. She's a nice lady. We talked about what happened at school today.'

My neck started to stiffen again. 'So does she hate me too?'

'No, of course not. You know, they have a very interesting background. Did you know that in Hungary they lived in a place called the Great Plain and ran a horseriding farm?'

'Horseriding farm? So ... they rode horses?'

'Of course. Hugo's mum said that Hugo was a very good rider. In fact, he could ride before he could walk.'

Ride before he could walk! I couldn't even walk before I could walk!

'Did she mention anything about bulls?'

Mum looked surprised. 'Why, as a matter of fact she did. Apparently Tabby is going to have a mechanical bull at her party and it's all Hugo can talk about.'

I bet.

I think I just discovered Hugo's secret.

'She said her son used to ride real bulls and he can't wait to show you kids how good he is.'

I bet he can't.

'And after the trouble you got into with Mr Mulcaster, young man, I think you should encourage Hugo to ride that bull well, and really cheer for him, make him feel special.'

Sure, Mum.

Like that was going to happen!

Mum didn't know the real Hugo like I did.

The HuGo everyonE sees.

The REAL HuGo

He was planning to embarrass me bad, making up a challenge he couldn't lose. AND he wanted Tabby to be his girlfriend! AND he had stolen my best friend!

There was no way I could beat him on the bull, even if the chicken did fly straight into my mouth.

More important than that though, Hugo was chasing Tabby. And she liked him! He was so smooth, and he was escorting her to her party!

I couldn't beat him at that either! I had no idea how to make a girl like me.

I decided to ask Dad because he had somehow made Mum like him even though he was mostly bald.

He said, 'Ah lad, now there's a question, one for the ages ... how do you make a girl like you?'

I had to wait for some time while his eyes searched the ceiling.

'Well,' started Dad, eventually. 'They've always been a mystery to me and God knows why your mother chose me. But one thing's for sure, son, you've got to get their attention, make that special girl notice you.'

All my parents told me was go to work.
I suppose that's what happens when you're a worker ant!

Dad seemed really chuffed that we had spoken about

girls, as if he'd been waiting to cross that off a list of all the things that fathers need to teach their sons ...

Actually, girls wasn't even on his list! In fact it was just a list of stuff he wanted me to learn so he wouldn't have to do it anymore. I think it's probably the worst Dad list I've ever seen, like where was teaching me to shave or fish or talk to girls?!

List of things to teach Fredd...

~~1 Wipe his bottom~~

2. Clean his room.

~~3 Walk the dog~~.

That night I was reading to Jessica as usual. We were reading nursery rhymes again and naturally there were gruesome ones ...

Rock-a-bye baby, in the treetop,
When the wind blows, the cradle will rock,
When the bough breaks, the cradle will fall,
And down will come baby, cradle, and all.

Okay, so here we have a baby crashing out of a tree. And you have to ask; who puts their baby in a treetop? Why not a low branch if you must put it in a tree? And why on a windy day?

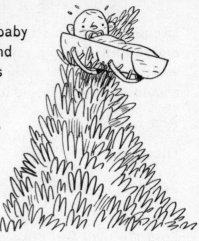

People sure were weird back then.

Jessica thought it was hilarious. I thought her head was going to fall off, she was laughing so much. I started laughing too, because when someone laughs it makes you laugh too, but then I stopped because I read something that was really important.

It was a rhyme about what girls were like. It was amazing. It was gold! With this information I could make Tabby like me for sure.

The rhyme was called, *What are Little Boys made of?*

What are little boys made of?
Snips and snails and puppy-dogs' tails,
That's what little boys are made of!
What are little girls made of?
Sugar and spice and all things nice,
That's what little girls are made of!

Sugar and spice and all things nice?

I know it's just a stupid rhyme but still, there was a clue in it. Like, it says that girls are nice and made of sugar and spice ... like lollies, so maybe I should get Tabby some lollies ...

And then it hit me!

Of course!

You don't give lollies to lollies.

The secret wasn't what girls are like, but what boys are like. Girls like boys, and they like them because they're boys. And boys are made of snips and snails and puppy-dogs' tails.

That's it!

If I wanted Tabby to like me then I had to ... to ... give her a snail?

That didn't sound right.

The dictionary told me that a snip was a *small irritating person*. It seemed weird that girls would like irritating boys, and snails ...

How romantic!

Hmm, I love snails!

Still, Dad said I had to get noticed, and that seemed to be pretty much what snips do, so it was all starting to make sense. I would try it out tomorrow.

That night I had a nightmare. I was at school talking to Tabby and everything was going well. She thought I was interesting, loads of fun, because I was running around like a puppy dog, like a snip, and we were having a great old time ...

When Hugo rode up on ... a horse!

On a brilliant white horse, like he was some kind of prince.

Hugo said to me, 'Hey Freddy, why don't you have any clothes on?'

I looked down and he was right! I didn't have any clothes on!

That made Tabby realise. She started pointing at me and laughing.

I was so embarrassed. And then, she jumped on the back of Hugo's horse and they rode away together ...

Together!

Leaving me at school with no clothes on and everyone laughing.

The next day, on the way to school, I must have checked whether I had clothes on at least ten times.

When I saw Tabby at school she was talking to some friends.

I said hi, but she ignored me. I think she was still annoyed about me running away. Time to try my snip experiment.

I put my bag down, picked up some little twigs and threw them at her.

She turned and told me to stop it, but I was a snip, so I kept doing it. I still couldn't see how this was going to make her like me, but what did I know? I had to try and it was kind of fun. I was trying to land them on the top of her head, and when I did I yelled, 'GOAL!'

Finally, she spun around and yelled,

'WHAT DO YOU WANT?!'

I wanted her to see me as the most interesting boy she knew.

'If I get enough twigs on there,' I said, pointing to her hair, 'birds might build a nest.'

'You are SO annoying!'

That was promising. A snip would like that. I kept running around her, lobbing sticks on the top of her head.

She yelled,

'WHY DON'T YOU JUST RUN AWAY? THAT'S WHAT YOU'RE GOOD AT!'

So, she was still mad about that ...

I should have said to her, 'Sorry, I shouldn't have run away, that was wrong', but I was in the middle of my experiment and snips don't say sorry.

I threw more sticks while Tabby swiped them off and kicked at me whenever I came too close.

Then she stopped trying, breathed in a deep breath and said, 'You can keep doing it if you like. I don't care. I don't care about you at all. You are the most irritating boy in the entire world!'

I was the most irritating boy in the entire world ...

YES! The perfect snip!

Remembering that the poem also talked about snails and puppy-dogs' tails, I decided to run around her pretending I was a puppy dog.

The other girls laughed but Tabby ignored me even when I started barking and whining.

She screamed all of a sudden,

'LEAVE ME ALONE!'

Hugo turned up. I checked to see if I was naked, because it was about now that Hugo rode off with Tabby on a horse.

Hugo stood right by her. 'Why don't you do what Tabby says, and leave her alone?'

I was not going to be a chicken this time. I could see his nose-picking finger was glistening from recent use.

'So, still picking your nose, I see. Tasty, was it?'

Hugo's eyes glistened with victory.

'You have lost! I have won Tabby and I will win on the bull! Accept that you have been beaten and LEAVE!'

He was pointing away, for me to leave. My voice was quiet, but strong.

'No chance,
Booger Boy.'

Hugo's eyes narrowed.
He was about to do
something, I'm not sure
what, but Tabby's shout
stopped everything.

On what?

If they eat it, that's wrong. If they flick it on the ground, that's ok. The I can eat it.

'That's it!'

Tabby pushed past Hugo to come between us.

'You boys care more about that stupid bull than you do about my birthday!'

'I care about you,' began Hugo.

'UH!' Tabby raised her hand to make him stop talking. 'And where do you get off calling me your girlfriend like I'm some kind of prize in your stupid competition?'

I don't think Hugo was ready for how angry Tabby was, which I think I can take some credit for.

Hugo started grovelling, 'You're much more than that to me, Tabby. I will be your escort and it will be a great honour for me ...'

Tabby pressed on, with a frown at Hugo. 'I'm not going to have that stupid bull at my party!'

'But you must!' Hugo splurted, shocked.

Tabby smiled dangerously. 'It's okay, Hugo. You can still escort me.'

Hugo really should have seen the danger. He actually thought he could win. 'If you want me to be your escort, then you have to have the bull at your party tomorrow, okay? End of discussion!'

Most everyone there winced at Hugo's words. If he'd looked at the Tabby Angryometer, he would have seen that he shouldn't have said anything.

'So, let me get this straight: you only want to escort me if the bull is there. You only want me to be your girlfriend to annoy Freddy. And, you think this discussion is over?'

Hugo was starting to realise his mistake, and was looking around for something to protect himself with.

Tabby snapped, sharp as a knife.

'This is my party and I can do what I want! And what I want is no **BULL!**'

No-one was ready for Hugo's response. I think he realised he wasn't going to talk his way out of it, so maybe shouting would work. He got right in Tabby's face.

'So what's the point of even going to your stupid party if there's no bull?'

Tabby stepped back in shock.

I jumped forward and pushed Hugo away. 'Hey! Back off!'

I shoved him away. Suddenly he was sounding whiny.

'But she's not going to have the bull there, so we can't have our challenge.'

I tried not to smile at that thought.

'It doesn't matter. We can do some other challenge, and like, why are we having a challenge anyway? I already said I was sorry. This challenge thing is stupid!'

'You're just chicken because you know you'll lose!'

I said, 'We don't need the bull to have fun. The party is for Tabby, and if you don't want to be there for her then ... then ... go have a snot sandwich.'

Hugo left, faster than a slippery finger sliding up a nostril.

'Thanks Freddy,' said Tabby. 'That was really nice of you.'

'That's okay, who needs a stupid bull at your party to have fun? We're all there for you.'

She smiled again, so I threw a few more sticks at her hair to make her like me even more.

For some reason that turned her smile into a stare that threatened death if another stick came her way.

'And,' she said, brushing the sticks away, 'because I know how much you want the mechanical bull there for your challenge, I'm going to tell Dad to make sure it is.'

What?

'No!' I cried. 'I mean ... thanks, Tabby, but you really don't have to. Hugo was so mean and it will make him pay for what he said if it's not there, so I don't think it should be.'

'But I know how much you want it too, Freddy, you want to be the champion rider and I want to reward you for being so nice.'

'It's okay, I don't mind.'

'Well, I do. I want to do something nice for you. It's my birthday and what I say goes.'

'Well ... thanks.' What else could I say?

The bell rang so we trudged off to class.

On the way, Scabs appeared. He checked out my fresh scabs from yesterday. 'Hmmm, coming along nicely. Those will stiffen up and start to fall off soon.'

He really was an expert at scabs.

Blocker turned up in the corridor outside class. Someone told him I said something mean to Hugo again. Great.

Blocker blew up straight away. 'I can't believe you did it again!'

I tried to explain but he wasn't listening. Hugo turned up so I ended it, saying, 'And I can't believe you hang with him!'

'And you,' I said to Hugo. 'Tabby is going to have the bull there tomorrow because I wanted it.'

'Then you'll lose!'

For the rest of the day Hugo kept giving me the hard stares and pointing a finger at me as if to say, *I'll get you*. I thought he should have thanked me for getting the mechanical bull back, but no chance of that.

That afternoon the Henry family set up the big tent in the park for Tabby's birthday. All the kids were down there watching.

I could see Cooper pointing to the rock I went over when I was practising for the bull. Cooper's finger traced the way I came through the trees and over the rocks and flying through the air. Everyone was cacking themselves, including Blocker and Hugo.

I went home.

I spoke to Dad that night about losing, because he's really good at it. He loses at golf all the time. His friends say that no-one can lose as well as he can. I suppose it's always good to be good at something.

I asked him what I should do, like should I fake having an injury or pretend I'm sick.

He said I should turn up and do my best. Typical Dad advice. Then he said that to hide how bad he was at golf he wore really flashy clothes that made him look like a good golfer.

That was amazing, because that's exactly what I was planning to do with my cowboy outfit.

Hmmm ... maybe I was doomed to be just like my dad!

That night I had another nightmare.

The worst one yet.

I was at school again. Mr Mulcaster was yelling at me. His eyes were going everywhere like a mad robot's and he was saying how much of a bully I was and why wasn't I more like Hugo. Naturally, once again I was completely naked!

Then I was in front of Hugo trying to apologise, only Hugo started to grow fangs and long hairy black legs and before I knew it, Hugo had turned into a huntsman spider.

It was Hugo's head on a huntsman!

He started chasing me. I was naked and being chased by a huge hairy long-legged huntsman Hugo spider!

I was trying to run as fast as I could but no matter how hard I tried, I just couldn't get past this slow-motion running, knowing that the Hugo spider was right behind me with fangs and goggly eyes, and everyone was laughing at me, pointing at my nakedness and not caring that this massive evil Hugo spider was about to eat me! I tried to run but I was stuck in the one spot. When at last I woke up I leapt to my feet, trembling, desperately looking for the spider.

I didn't fall asleep again that night.

It was the worst dream I'd ever had. Or was it a dream? Maybe I was just seeing the future. Hugo was hunting me and there was nowhere to run.

The next day I went over to Blocker's so I could talk to him. I wanted to tell him what Hugo was really like. He wasn't there. He had spent the night at Hugo's and his mum said they were going straight to Tabby's party from there.

I missed Blocker being my friend. I suppose he had more in common with someone who used to live near Russia and who understood his sayings.

I went to the party by myself. I packed a bag with my cowboy outfit in it and rode down to the park.

There were people
everywhere. I couldn't
believe how big the party
was. Tabby's family was
huge. There must have
been a thousand people
in the park.

Party! Let's get
to the food!

I want
chicken!

I went straight to the big tent, because I've been
to parties before and I've learned that it's always
best to get the food first, before it runs out.

I met Scabs and Cooper there. We ate some
lollies and a sausage sandwich and went on the
jumping castle, which was more like a jumping
city. It was huge and we had a crazy time, but I
couldn't stop
thinking about
the mechanical
bull.

I went down
to have a look.
There was a
long line waiting for
a turn and a crowd was
watching and cheering as the
riders flew off in all directions.

The man running it was saying with a
wink that ol' Buckaroo was in a mighty
cranky mood today.

And there on a table next to him was a blue medallion that read Buckaroo Blue: Champion Rider.

It was going to hurt to see that on Hugo.

Everyone who tried to ride ol' Buckaroo said the same thing: it was too hard to hang onto the rope when the bull sped up.

Cooper had a turn and lasted about ten seconds before he went flying.

Most people flew off when the speed was on Hang On.

The man said you had to do more than just hang on. You had to move with the bull. He said you would need to be a proper bull rider to last longer than ten seconds on See You Later.

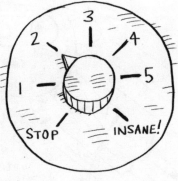

You would need to be someone like Hugo.

I should have had a practice right then but I knew I would be thrown off like everyone else, and I wasn't ready to know that yet. This little piggy still wanted to dream about acorns.

Hugo and Blocker appeared together as usual. I didn't feel like putting up with Hugo right now. I hid. Ol' Buckaroo was set up really close to the tree with the bush around the bottom of it where I'd hidden from Hugo before, so I snuck in there again.

Hugo was walking around like he owned the place. He was beaming, calling out, telling everyone to come and watch him. A massive crowd gathered to watch and he was amazing. He rode the bull like a real rodeo rider. He went all the way to the Awesome Rider speed which made the crowd go nuts. They gave him a huge cheer and the operator said that Hugo would get the Buckaroo Blue unless someone could beat that.

I left my bag in the bush. I wasn't ready to get in my cowboy gear yet and face Hugo. I wanted to enjoy the party for a while first.

I went back to the big tent. Tabby was there next to a mountain of presents. When she saw me she ran up and dragged me over to show me.

'Look Freddy, this one's from you. What is it?'

'It's a new car.'

'Pfff.'

'Open it and see.'

I would have preferred a new car.

I would prefer chicken.

It was two red scrunchies. I didn't have very much money.

'I thought red might look nice in your hair,' I said.

'Really?' She put them on her pigtails. 'I love them!'

We went jumping on the castle.

We were having a great time until I saw Hugo watching me from the edge. I had to talk to him eventually, so I went over and said, 'We don't have to do this challenge. I know you're the best, so let's just have fun.'

Hugo said if I didn't challenge him, then I was a chicken.

I told him that I saw him earlier and that he was amazing, way better than me, and so what was the point?

He smiled darkly, 'So you are a chicken!'

Plenty of people were listening.

'No!'

'Then we ride.'

He stuck his hand out to shake on our challenge. I didn't want to shake it, I knew where his fingers had been. But a lot of people were watching so I had to.

Did someone say chicken?

Blocker was there too and he said, 'I'll be the timer.'

Tabby whispered in my ear, 'You make sure you beat him, Freddy.'

'Sure. No problem.'

I decided I wouldn't put my cowboy gear on. I would have a quick go and get thrown off. Hugo would win and that would be it, see you later Hugo, well done and good luck with the rest of your life.

Hugo called me over to the waiting line and yelled, 'Sir, we have a challenger for Champion Rider. He thinks he's better than I am!'

All eyes went to me and some of them started laughing.

Hugo yelled again, as if it was hilarious,

'BETTER THAN ME! WHAT A LOSER!'

That was it. Hugo had been pushing me around long enough. If he wanted a show, then a show he'd get. I'd get into my cowboy gear and carry on so much that they'd love me for the show. Like Dad said, if you're going to lose, do it in style. Hugo might win the Blue, but I'd win the crowd.

'Give me five minutes!'

I ran into the crowd before doubling back and crawling quickly under the bush so no-one saw me.

I grabbed my bag and pulled out my cowboy gear. There wasn't much room in there to change, and I didn't want to shake the bush or people on the outside might investigate, so I was real careful taking off my clothes.

Oops ...

I realised I wasn't wearing any undies and I hadn't packed any in the bag. Like it didn't matter so much but it did mean I had to get totally naked.

I took off my clothes and had a horrible feeling that the bush would suddenly fall down and everyone would turn around and see me standing there naked.

Creepy.

I grabbed my pants to put on, only something furry touched my hand ...

I looked down ...

Oh, so that's how you tell boys and girls apart.

So why do they hide it?

103

And there on my hand, was the biggest, hairiest, meanest-looking spider I had ever seen. A huntsman!

And it was on me!

I flung my pants down and flicked my hand to get it off. It landed on my clothes, at my feet! I backed up against the tree, scraping at my hand where the spider had been.

Another huntsman crawled out of my bag!

Out of my bag!

The spiders started walking. Towards me! On their creepy long black hairy legs.

My nightmare was coming true! Naked and chased by spiders!

I had to get out, get away, right now! I had to go now! But the only way out of the bush was right into the crowds of people.

I would be naked in front of hundreds of people ...

I heard my name.

'Freddy, where are you?'

It was Hugo. Others were calling as well and some of them were right next to me but I couldn't say anything.

I heard Hugo's voice above them all.

'You're a chicken, Tangles, a chicken!'

Maybe I was, but it wasn't because of him. It was spiders. They were so big and so hairy and way too close and getting closer and who knew how many more were hiding in my bag!

I hate spiders, too.

It's hard to love something that poisons you and sucks your guts out.

I took a deep breath and planned my path. I would burst through the bush and run as fast as I could through the whole crowd, all the way home ... naked!

I pushed up hard against the tree for leverage. Time to go. Time to run ... and then I thought ... the tree ...

I could go up the tree!

I could climb. No! I hated climbing. I was afraid of heights! But ... if I climbed just a little way up then I would escape the spiders and I wouldn't have to run out naked.

There was a fork in the tree that wasn't very high. I could get there easily and I would still be hidden by the bush.

I pulled myself up onto the fork. The bush still covered me if I sat down. I felt a little dizzy being off the ground but I was sitting and more importantly, I was away from the spiders.

I heard the man at the bull say, 'Okay, Hugo, your turn, let's see you go for the record.'

Blocker said, 'I'll time you anyway. He still might turn up.'

Not likely. I wasn't going anywhere. I was going to stay right where I was until the party was over, everyone had gone home, the sun had set, the moon had set and the police had stopped looking for me.

Then something changed all that. Something that I couldn't believe.

One of the spiders started climbing the tree!

It was on the ground and I was in the tree and that was good for everyone but no, this was a huntsman spider!

I could see its little beady eyes staring straight up at me and I'm sure it said, 'I'm coming to get you, Freddy Tangles.' I swear it said it! And then the other one crawled onto the tree as well! They were both coming for me!

New plan! I had to jump into the bush. It would make a huge noise. Everyone would turn around and see me naked and I would be stuck hanging in the scratchy thorny branches and they would all have to help me out of the bush, while I'm totally starkers!

I would look like the most stupid naked chicken person there ever was.

But there was no other choice!

Unless ... I could climb higher up the tree. There was a branch ...

The spiders were coming closer. I had to do something. No time to freeze like I did on the bike. I had to make a decision! Everyone was looking at Hugo. He was climbing onto the bull and they were cheering.

Now was my chance. The branch above me was really thick and had some leaves where maybe I could hide until night-time.

Okay! I started to climb. If anyone turned and looked up right now they would see me naked.

This really was turning into something worse than any nightmare I'd ever had ... stuck naked high up a tree with spiders chasing me and Hugo embarrassing me below on the mechanical bull.

I looked down to see him getting on the bull and nearly fell with the sudden dizziness of being so high.

Don't look down!

I gripped the trunk really hard, turned my

eyes back to the tree and
climbed until I reached
the big branch. When I
got there I wedged myself
against the trunk and
closed my eyes.

My heart was beating so hard ...

Thump thump thump

At least I was safe from the spiders ... or was I?

I had to check. I held on tight, looked down,
and couldn't believe it ... the spiders were still
coming! They were so close that if I wanted to,
I could have reached down and touched them!

The spiders stopped and looked at me. I think
they were wondering which part of me they
wanted to eat first. They could eat whatever
they wanted because it was all there naked and
waiting, like some kind of takeaway tree tasty.

I think I would have cried right then if I wasn't
so scared.

My fingernails had dug themselves into the tree
trunk. I had to move, get away, but I was so high
and whenever I looked out my vision went swirly.
I couldn't climb higher, I couldn't reach the next
branch anyway. Maybe I should just jump ... I
might break my leg but at least I would be free.

Or I could move along the branch ... to the canopy of leaves at the end of it.

If I crawled along the branch I would be hidden from the people below and I could hide there until night-time. It was a chance, and if I had to jump, it wasn't any worse than jumping from here!

Surely the spiders wouldn't follow me all the way out there.

Surely!

The branch went out over the crowd towards Hugo on the mechanical bull.

I pulled my fingernails out of the trunk and started inching along the branch. My heart hammered in my chest. I was sweating and scrunching my eyes so all I could see was a little bit of the branch in front of me and not the sky or the ground or anything.

The further I went along the branch, the skinnier and bouncier it got. Luckily, Hugo had started his riding so they were all staring at him and making heaps of noise with their cheering.

They were yelling,

'Go Hugo! You can do it! Ride 'em, cowboy!'

I made it to the leaves.

There was no big trunk out there to lean on. All I could do was sort of lie down on the skinny branches, and not move.

I kept my eyes closed.

I could hear the whir of the mechanical bull and the cheering of the crowd right below me.

I started to wonder about the spiders. Had they followed me out? In my nightmares they never gave up, no matter how hard I tried to get away.

Hugo was still riding below. I heard Blocker call out, 'Sixty seconds!'

The man at the mechanical bull yelled out, 'The **speed is now Awesome Rider!**'

I heard the mechanical bull speed up and the crowd cheer even louder.

I lay there with my eyes shut tight but I couldn't stop thinking about the spiders. Were they still following? Would I feel them creep onto my feet? I couldn't stand it. I had to know. I had to look!

I tilted my head and looked back down the branch ...

And there they were. Right there!

I started to cry. I couldn't help it. It burst out of me like someone squeezing a sponge.

They were still hunting me. Their creepy hairy legs and fangs were getting closer and closer and I had nowhere else to go. It didn't matter how hard I tried, how far I climbed, or how fast I tried to run, I could never escape the spiders, never!

And then I fell out of the tree.

I'm not sure how it happened. I think I just forgot that I was in a tree ...

I was going to land straight on Hugo.

Naked!

It was a weird moment. Time seemed to slow right down. It was like I was floating in the air.

It must have only been a second or two but in that time I saw so many faces ... Scabs, Cooper, Tabby and Block. I could see the jumping castle and the sausage sizzle. I could even see that there were only a few sausages left.

I was about to crash into Hugo when he got unbalanced and was thrown off the bull just as I landed ... on the bull!

Everyone was looking at me and I was totally
naked and the spiders were right above my head
and they would jump down for sure because they
never give up, so I grabbed the rope on the bull
and kicked at its sides to gallop me away.

I cried madly,

'GO! GO!'

It was really bucking and swerving but I didn't care, I needed to get away fast and it was moving fast!

'HEEYAR! HEEYAR!'

The bull was really flying ... only it wasn't going anywhere. It was like me running in my dream, when the spiders are coming and I'm running but I can't get away!

I screamed, **'Faster! Faster!'**

I heard the man yell out, 'Okay, it's now on Totally Mad!'

And the bull just went crazy, but I still wasn't going anywhere, I still couldn't escape and the spiders were coming down for sure, like I was Little Miss Muffet, sitting on her tuffet, trying to get away!

But I couldn't! And everyone knew it and they were laughing at me naked!

I kicked at the bull again and again. It had to go faster, I had to get away from the people and the spiders. I screamed,

'Faster! Faster!'

And the man screamed back, **'It's now on top speed!'**

Everything turned
into a blur. It was
INSANE!

There was
so much
noise and I
was flying
around but
the people
were still
there and
the spiders
were still
above me.

I couldn't
get away!

I can never
get away ...
never go fast enough!

And then the bull slowed down.

I yelled, 'No! No!'

I didn't want it to stop. I was still naked and the
spiders were still above me and the people were
still laughing at me ...

No, they were cheering ... they were
cheering!

Blocker came over with a picnic rug and put it around my shoulders. The man who worked the bull came up to us.

He was saying, 'I've never seen anything like that, young man. No-one has ever ridden ol' Buckaroo at the top speed and stayed on.'

I couldn't get off the bull. The man had to pry my fingers off the rope and my knees from the saddle.

I heard Blocker say, 'You won, Freddy, no-one has ever ridden a bull that well.'

'I was trying to get away,' I said. 'Are the spiders still coming?'

'Spiders?' Blocker put his arm around me and led me away. 'No spiders here, Freddy. Come on, let's go sit down for a while.'

I stiffened. 'No, we can't!'

'You mean the spiders?'

'No!'

I remembered something from when I was falling from the tree. 'There's something we absolutely have to do before we sit down.'

'What?'

'This way, quick!'

'What is it?'

I pushed through the surging crowd. So many back-slaps and high fives!

'Quick, Block, follow me. There's no time!'

'What? What is it?'

'When I was falling, I saw that there were only a few sausages left. Are you hungry?'

Blocker laughed. 'Me? I'm always hungry.'

It was nice having Block by my side again.

'Where's Hugo?' I asked.

'He took off after you won.'

'Why didn't you go too? I thought you were like best friends now.'

'Best friends? No way.'

'But you hang with him all the time now.'

'I was trying to help him. He wasn't fitting in and I thought it was because he was from Hungary. I thought I could help him, and part of that was staying away from you. But, as it turns out, it wasn't because he was from Hungary, it's because he isn't a very nice person.'

'So you don't like him that much?'

'Not even a bit. He gets angry all the time and he's always thinking of how to make people do what he wants them to.'

'Don't I know it! Well, it's good to have you back.'

'I wasn't ever gone. I was just trying to help someone.'

'There's an old Russian saying ...'

There are heaps of old Russian sayings! Only it wasn't Blocker who said it.

Tabby hustled up from behind. 'Do not search for a friend in time of need, for a true friend shall find you.'

Blocker frowned. 'That doesn't sound very Russian.'

'Ah well. Who else would have thought to find a blanket for Freddy?'

Blocker laughed. 'Almost everyone there if they saw what I saw!'

'Very funny.'

She gave him a kiss on the cheek, right there in front of everyone.

I must say I felt a little bit jealous, but Blocker deserved it.

'And you!' Tabby shook her head at me. 'It's my birthday and you're not wearing any clothes ...'

'Freddy's in his birthday suit!' yelled Cooper, catching up.

I dropped my eyes. How stupid was I? Tabby must think I was the stupidest boy alive.

She leaned over and said, 'That was the bravest, most magnificent thing I have ever seen, ever!'

And with that she planted a kiss on me too. Only not on my cheek ... right on my lips!

People cheered again.
I blushed really
badly and didn't
know what to say.

Block reminded
me about the
sausages so we
headed off fast.
We left Tabby there. I
wasn't running away this
time. Well, okay, I sort
of was because I was
embarrassed, like what do you do after a girl
kisses you?

We saw Hugo up near the sausages. He was
picking his nose and eating it.

'At least Hugo didn't take the last sausages,' I said.

Blocker was grim. 'Didn't need to. Brought his own
food.' I went over to him. 'Hey Hugo, nice riding.'

He was with a couple of guys
I didn't know very well.

'You cheated!' he bleated.
'I had to jump off because
you were going to land on me.'

'Yeah, he had to jump!'
said one of his friends.

'And you weren't wearing clothes!' said the other.

Blocked gave Hugo a friendly slap on the back. 'Well, it's good to see you found some friends, Hugo. Now you don't have to hang with us.'

He turned to me. 'Let's go Freddy, we've got some proper eating to do.'

We grabbed the last sausages.

Scabs turned up with my clothes and to tell the truth, I put them on reluctantly. I was getting used to walking around with only a blanket on, with everyone cheering me wherever I went.

Tabby called out to me, 'Freddy come over! It's time for the presentation!'

On the way over, Blocker asked, 'So are you going to go around with Tabby now?'

'I dunno,' I said, unsettled at the idea. 'If she asks me I will.'

'Hugo reckons that boys can ask girls as well.'

I shook my head doubtfully. 'I've never seen that happen.'

'I'm pretty sure boys can't ask until it's time to get married,' Blocker agreed.

Tabby ran to me, grabbed my hand and pulled me to a spot in front of the mechanical bull. The man had the medal in his hand and said, 'Lad, I ain't never seen anyone ride ol' Buckaroo like that ever! Not only here but anywhere!'

He pinned the medal on.

Cooper yelled out, 'Just as well you're wearing clothes now, Freddy, or that would have hurt!'

Everyone laughed. I looked down at the medal. The Buckaroo Blue. The best thing I've ever won! It said I was a Champion Rider but I wasn't too sure about that. Maybe I was really a chicken.

Like, I know I won and everyone was calling me the Champ, but if I hadn't been so scared about spiders and heights and not wearing clothes, I would have lost for sure.

Champ or Chicken?

How about Champion Chicken?

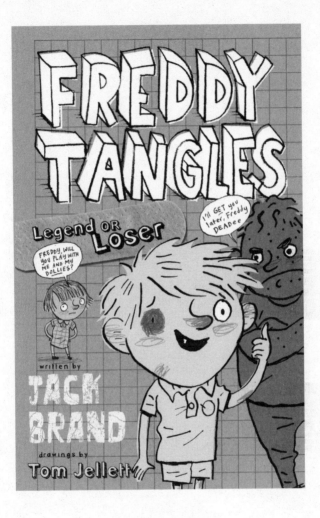

OUT NOW